THE BIRDS OF CALAMITY

WHY WE MET

SULEKHA GUJJAR

Copyright © Sulekha Gujjar
All Rights Reserved.

This book has been published with all efforts taken to make the material error-free after the consent of the author. However, the author and the publisher do not assume and hereby disclaim any liability to any party for any loss, damage, or disruption caused by errors or omissions, whether such errors or omissions result from negligence, accident, or any other cause.

While every effort has been made to avoid any mistake or omission, this publication is being sold on the condition and understanding that neither the author nor the publishers or printers would be liable in any manner to any person by reason of any mistake or omission in this publication or for any action taken or omitted to be taken or advice rendered or accepted on the basis of this work. For any defect in printing or binding the publishers will be liable only to replace the defective copy by another copy of this work then available.

THE BIRDS OF CALAMITY

MUMBAI, INDIA

Evening 5 PM, 15 March 2018,

Priya (Advocate) is very enthusiastic girl and she living in mumbai with her father and aunt …this is her small world, her small family and her friends, today she is very happy celebrating her 28th birthday with her friends in Blue REDDISON HOTEL Mumbai.

(After that she started going out of the hotel by saying goodbye to her friends after celebrating her birthday)

Suddenly a bomb exploded in the hotel, and due to the bomb blast in the hotel, there was a ruckus in the hotel.

Priya and her friends just escape from the hotel

And the police came outside the hotel and many people lost their lives due to the bomb blast, many children lost their lives in many families.

Priya felt very sad knowing all this as she returned to her house with her friends but she could not come out of the shock.

(After reaching home Priya turned on TV)

And News was coming on TV that behind this bomb blast is the hand of Indian Gangster (Nirvaan Khan) (age 34) who living in Dubai who is commanding this matter from Dubai itself.

(Priya immediately goes to the police station and meet Sub –
inspector (Rakesh Shinde) (age 45))

Priya :- Such a big bomb has exploded, so many people have lost
their lives and you are not even doing anything on this matter.

Sub- inspector: - Our police department will not be able to do
anything in this case, even before this many cases are registered on
Gangster (Nirvaan khan) but till date no one has been able to catch
him.

Priya :- (shocked) but Why?

Sub - insperctor:- He (Nirvaan Khan) has huge political power
connection in india, he is very cunning man, He lives in Dubai and
commands the political power from there and till date it is very
difficult to catch him.

Sub – inspector: - (Continued...) Our police Department has full
confidence and proofs that this Gangster (Nirvaan Khan (age 34)) is
behind this bomb blast but we are helpless. because He has huge
political power connection in india. We don't even know what he that
looks like because he deleted all his records from our department.

Priya: - But why is he (Nirvaan khan) doing all this, what will he get by
killing so many innocent people?

Sub-Insperctor: - He does out of his hatred, He hates this city
because his father was a police officer in our own department who
was sued for false bribery, and because of this embarrassment his
father committed suicide.

Priya :- shocked! And than ......

Sub – insperctor : - (continued).... His mother also died due to this shock, he had lost his everything overnight, in this anger he first planted a bomb on the district court in 2002....and after that he is unstopable.

Priya :- (sympathize) I agree that very bad has happened to him, but so many innocent lives have been lost and he will have to answer for that

(Priya asked the sub-inspector for the file of all previous criminal records of Nirvaan Khan so that she could re-open all his Case.)

(And the next day, Priya opens the criminal cases of Nirvaan Khan and files the Criminal case or PIL against him in the court.)

ABU HAIL, DUBAI

(Nirvaan Khan was busy in his corporate meeting while his Manager (shoaib khan) came and told him that)

Nirvaan khan: - what happened? can, t you see I am in meeting.

Manager: - Sorry! Sir it was very important so I called you.

Nirvaan Khan: - tell me what happened?

Manager:- Sir, a court notice has come in your name at your home in India, in which a girl named Advocate Priya, she has filled a Criminal case or PIL against you, and your criminal case has been re - opened too.

Nirvaan Khan :- so what! What will she harm me, the silly child is still learning, she is wasting her time and you should handle this matter on your own, this thing should not come to me.

Manager :- ok sir .

After few days, (his Manager came to Nirvaan Khan and tell)

Manager :- Sir! You will have to go to India for a once, after talking about you to all political parties, that everyone said that we will not be able to help so much in the matter of the court, just once you will have to become appear.

Nirvaan Khan :- (with cunning smile)....ok i will go to india but this game is started by that girl i will end this game.

I will shown that girl (Adv Priya) , that she has put her hand in the mouth of the lion.

MUMBAI, INDIA

On Monday 25 march morning 11AM (Mumbai)

(Nirvaan Khan arrived at Mumbai airport and went straight to his hotel from there. After reaching the hotel, he called all his politician friends for a meeting in his room and asked who is this girl and why has she filed a case against me,)

A Politician friend : she is an ordinary girl who is 28 years old and she is a lawyer.

Nirvaan Khan :- Was it so important for me to appear in court that I had to come here from Dubai?

Politian friend :- yes sir ! that's how our constitution work hope you understand.

Nirvaan Khan:- ok ,, I understood ...My trial date is after a week, I will be present in the court after a week on 2 april 2018.

(The next day Nirvaan Khan changes his name like a normal Man, with fake name (Akshay) and fake indentity (intern) goes to court and goes to Priya's cabin and says hello ma'am, I have come in.)

Priya :- yes! Coming

Nirvaan Khan :- Good Morning ma`am! my name is Akshay. I am a lawyer and I have completed my bachelor degree this year and a friend of mine has suggested me to do intership under you.

Priya :- I do not want to keep anyone on intership because I do not have enough time to hire a person because I am working on very important cases , you go to someone else please

Nirvaan Khan :- ma`am Please! Allow me, to do intership under you because some of my friends have heard a lot about you, ... please

Priya :- Please you go, you are wasting my time, I do not have time, thank you, do internship with someone else.

(After this Priya closed the cabin and went on lunch with her friend in a restaurant.)

(While Priya was having lunch with her friends, Nirvaan Khan was calling her in gesture outside of the restraurant)

Priya`s friend :- Who is this boy who is calling you from outside the restraurant with such gestures do you have a boyfriend!

Priya :- No, he is not my boyfriend , This boy I met in court today told me that I want to do internship with me, I refused and he came here following me.

Priya`s friend :- ooo kk! But he is so cute,

Priya :- shut up , I am not interested,

Priya`s friend ;- I'm calling that boy inside the to have lunch with us.

Priya :- no please no ...

Priya`s friend :- I don't know I am calling him to join us for lunch.

(Priya`s friend call Nirvaan khan for having lunch with them and he came and they interduced with each other).

(After having lunch, all the friends start going to their respective homes, then Priya starts going alone to her house after saying goodbye to her friends, Nirvaan Khan asked to drop her to home.)

Priya :- ok lets walk ..

Nirvaan Khan :- why walk ? I have my own car...

Priya :-I know but .... I like to walk and roam at night, so I can see the beauty of mumbai city closely with my eyes .

Nirvaan Khan:- (smiling) you know, you are very different and strange girl. Ok let's walk!

(both go for a long walk)

Priya :- tell me something about you!

Nirvaan Khan :- I was born in Mumbai and where do I live, I was very close to my mom and dad, I grew up listening stories to my grandmother.And My grandmother used to tell me new- new stories about of king and queens.

Priya :- oh Really! I love to listen stories ... please tell one of the story which your grandmother used tell me ...(insists)

Nirvaan Khan :- oookkkk! Alright, I'll try it because I remember some hazy stories like the stories my grandmother used to tell me.

Priya :- please ..

Nirvaan Khan :- ok the story began ...Once upon a time there was a king, there was a queen, and queen was very beautiful. one day, when the king went hunting, both of you have met, both of them fell in love, and........

Priya :- oh nice! and ......than next....please continue...(excited)

Nirvaan Khan :- I remember this story only this much, I will remember it further, I will definitely tell you.

Priya :- oh no! its ok but promise whenever you remember the story you will definitely tell me the story.

Nirvaan Khan :- ok promise!...i will definitely tell you furthur story...

Priya :- thank you!

Nirvaan Khan :- so can i join you for internship from tomorrow

Priya :- (smiling) you are very smart! Ok sure ...

Nirvaan Khan :- thanks ...

(On the way, after drop Priya, Nirvaan went to her hotel saying good bye to her there.)

Priya and Nirvaan start missing each other after you go to there room..suddenly Nirvaan message to Priya on whatsapp ..

Nirvaan Khan :- (message on whatsapp).... Till date, I have not talked so much to anyone that I especially talk about my personal things that this night has become more beautiful for me too, this night was very special ..that I come to know ..that mumbai city is so beautiful ...only because of you, ,,thank you

Priya :- for me too ... this night was beautiful ... ok good night.

Nirvaan Khan :- good night...

(The very next day Nirvaan comes to Priya's cabin and Priya is busy in some cases.)

Nirvaan Khan :- (smiling) its seems like you are working on important case.

Priya :- yeah! I am working on important case, case about hotel blue Raddison bomb blast......and.. after 2 days i have hearing in court.

Nirvaan Khan :- (curious) may! I read this case file for once.

(After reading case file)

Nirvaan Khan :- to whom this case about do you know this person ?

Priya :- No, I do not know this person, I have not seen him, nor do I have any photo or picture Table 1of him, because he did not allow any of his photos to remain in his records, he has erased all the evidence.

Nirvaan Khan : (feel relax) you are so boring forget this case, do you Tomorrow is my birthday, tomorrow I want to spend my whole day with you, I want to celebrate my birthday with you.

Priya :- oh Really! Sure ....tomarrow is your day ..

THE LOVE CONFESSION

(the birthday celebration At Dinner)

Priya :- (excited) Hey, you remembered that story of your grandmother, story of the king and queen.

Nirvaan :- yeah! i remember....

Priya :- Tell me what happened will next in the story of king and queen ?

Nirvaan :- (see in her eyes) Till now, ever since the king has seen the queen, the king is still lost in the queen's eyes....

Priya :- (smiling and feel shy) yeah Sure, ha ha ha very funny....

Nirvaan Khan :- (now its my turn) ...I have so much curiosity about that what do you think of me what do you like in me now?

Priya :- (smiling and amaze) I think , I starting like you.

Nirvaan Khan :- Really! I am so lucky ,

Priya :- (continued..) I like specially your eyes the talking eyes flashing from eyes, deep eyes.

Nirvaan Khan :- (constantly look at Priya) No one has ever known me so deeply, like so you know me.

Priya :- now your turn .. tell me what do you like about me ?

Nirvaan Khan :- Everything about me is like yours ora and your independence, your intellectuality, I have met the girl like as you ...

Nirvaan Khan :- ...(after hold his breatyh looking at Priya and go closer to her and tell) .. I love you

Priya :- (heart beat become louder she replied) .. I love you too.. and forever ..

Priya :- continued(looking into his eyes)...I love you too .(Because with this boring life of mine, from court to house to court you have brought a beautiful turn in life.)

Nirvaan Khan :- (Holding Priya in his arms), I can't believe that I am so lucky .

(And both spend hours and hours of beautiful moments with each other)

Priya :- We should go home It's been a long night and tomorrow morning at 10:00, I have an important court case hearing.

Nirvaan Khan :- (kissed Priya`s forehead) ok .. lets go …. And all the very best for tomarrow case

Priya :- thank you

(You both say goodbye and go to his room.)

(On the day of court trail in morning on 2 april 2018)

Early in the morning, Priya was trying to file the case (Hotel Blue Reddison bomb blast) , which she was not getting, she was so panic that why she could not find the file after searching a lot but she could not find the file…

Priya Was working very hard to file find and become so panic , if she does not get that file today, then she will not be able to step in the court, if she goes to the court without a that file, she will lose her in straight away…

COURT TRAIL

Priya :- Your Honor! I am working on the case yet my work is not completed, please give me the next date on this matter.

Judge :- No! I Can't give you the next date in this case because you haven't even submitted this file with us yet.

Priya :- (Hopeless) your honour! Please try to understand ……..

Judge :- No! your case is dissmed now ..

(She left the court room with huge disappointed and sad because she had lost everything she had been working on that case for so long)

(after that Priya got call on her mobile from an unknown number and she picked up the call,)

Priya :- (in hopless mood) hello! Who is this ?

Nirvaan khan :- (in bold voice and being sarcastic) Nirvaan khan ... the Accuse of your case ...the Gangster ... don't you recognize me ..(continued)..ok ....(sarcastic) let's introduced myself in another way ... (hello miss Adv Priya ... I am your's 3 days fake lover Akshay ....)

Priya :- (Shocked and emotionally scriming)...you....fraud..coward.....

Niran khan :- (sarcastic) I totally understand...its ok ...(more sarcastic) I have heard that you have lost today case because the case file was lost from you, (laugh) ....

Priya :- (shocked and Scrime) .. So you stole that case File...

Nirvaan Khan :- (Laugh) Not bad! ...I guess you are a smart advocate ... you guess right miss Priya ......

Nirvaan Khan :- (continued...laughing and sarcastic) Yes, I have your case file and I have stolen your case file , I have some burnt pieces of that file ...now I will parcel to you.. Nirvaan Khan worry ...afterall you arev working on this case for so long ... (laugh)...

Priya :- (broken inside emotionally)...I hate you..

Nirvaan Khan: - (more sarcastically) .. oh Really! Thank you ...

Nirvaan Khan :- (sarcastically)... I am at Airport right now ...Now in half an hour my flight will land in Dubai, I will go back to Dubai,..... before I go to Dubai what happened next with King & Queen in my grandmother's story....

Priya :- (angry) I know ...that King was Coward ...

Nirvaan Khan :- (Laughing sarcastically)... I am telling you what happened next in story.....once there was a king and a queen , King and Queen met King, and the queen fell in love with the king, The king went away betraying the queen, now the queen left alone with her broken heart and her sad stories...(laughing)

Priya :- (emotinally) ..you cheater .... I hate you ...

Nirvaan khan :- I Hope we will never met again...good bye

(Nirvaan khan went to dubai) ....

DUBAI

(In the evening, Nirvaan was sitting in his room, using laptop an checking Priya's social media profile on laptop and his best friend (Raqeeb)(age 35) came to meet him.....)

Friend (Raqeeb) :- Your manager told me that after coming from India. you had 5 to 6 meetings on board, you canceled all the meetings, you spend time alone...you are not paying attention to any work ... are you fine?

Nirvaan :- yeah! I am fine .... What about you ?

Friend (Raqeeb) :- No, you are not fine... who is this girl, whose social media profile you have open in laptop....

Nirvaan :- (trying to ignore) she is nobody... she is just an ordinary girl from India.... I met to her in India ...that's it ...

Friend (Raqeeb) :- (curious)... Oh Really! I don't think she is just an ordinary girl.... since you came from India, i am noticing you have changed ...

Friend (Raqeeb) :- I think you have you fallen in love with her.. you are in love my friend ....you are in love

Nirvaan :- (with heavy heart and with watery eyes) ... I don't know about love .....I don`t know how love happens, all I know is that since I came to Dubai from India, I have not been able to live in peace even once, I am missing her, ...

Nirvaan :- (continued)...I am missing her so much .... I Feeling like flying back to India now and telling her how much I missing her ...and I fall for her ...

Friend (Raqeeb) :- (hold Nirvaan) I think you should talk to that girl and you should come back to India....now you should take some rest...

Nirvaan :- (with deeply analysis) you are right ! I should go back to india...Because my body has come to Dubai but my mind and heart have been left in India.

Friend (Raqeeb) :- ooo that`s great .....go back to india and meet that girl again and tell her that you are fallen for her ......you love her ..

Nirvaan :- (with his cunning smile)... raqeeb my friend .....you have been my friend for so many years, so I still don't know me and understood me that I am not made for love... love is not my cup of tea.

Friend (Raqeeb) :- (curious with thinking).. what!.. I didn't understand... then why you are going back to india ....

Nirvaan :- (continued with cunning smile) ...I am going back to India to kill that girl (Priya) there.

Friend (Raqeeb) :- (Shocked) ... but you love her ...

Nirvaan :- (stopping raqeeb) yes, I love her... That's why that girl(Priya) has become my weakness, she is like feeling is growing inside me, and this feeling pulls me to go back India again .....that's why I have to kill that girl because she has become my weakness...

Friend (Raqeeb) :- (Shocked and blank) ...I don't understand you why are you doing all this?... why it is necessary to kill that girl?...

Nirvaan :- (with deep analysis) raqeeb my friend ...remember! 12 years ago, when I lost my parents in India, I had only one weakness left in India, that was our old house, I had set our house on fire too... so that no weakness could drag me to India... and I came in Dubai...

Nirvaan :- that girl has become my weakness and I do not leave any weakness behind me...Before this weakness destroys me, I want to end this weakness so I have to killed her... this is part of my nature..

Friend (raqeeb) :- (Shocked) ...you are impossible man .....

Nirvaan : - yes! I am impossible ...you know me better...

Friend (Raqeeb) :- you were always stubborn like this, even you will not understand my explanation but in the end I want to say "When a person is living in so much hatred, he first likes himself in hatred".

(and his friend (Raqeeb) leave, After his friend leaves, Nirvaan calls his manager and says that do my ticket to go to India tomorrow.)

Manager :- Sir you are going to India, but tomorrow you have very important meetings.

Nirvaan :- Cancel all the meetings and get my ticket to go to India tommarrow.

Manager :- ok sir .... Sure ...

(Nirvaan call Priya in india.. and pick up the phone)

Priya :- hello ! who is this ?

Nirvaan :- (slowly) its me Nirvaan khan ... how are you ?

Priya :- (Hurtly) why did you called me ?

Nirvaan :- For once please forget about that case, can we reunite and can I meet with you, with my true identity as Nirvaan khan .Will you accept me as I am ?

Priya :- (Emotionally) .. okkk .. I am waiting for you here (India) .. please come soon ... I can't wait to see you come soon... and I love you so much ...

Nirvaan :- I am coming to india tommarrow in evening ... and I will meet ...there ..

Priya :- (Emotionally) I am waiting ...

Nirvaan :- And Remembered! grandmother's queen and king story was left still incomplete...

Priya :- Yeah ...Remember, so what happened next in king and queen story ?...

Nirvaan :- In king and queen story .... The king tried a lot to live, without the queen but he could not live without the queen. Now the king wants to come back to his queen...

Priya :- (Emotional and with smile).. even the queen is incomplete without her king...please come back ..

Nirvaan :- Tomorrow evening at 4:00 o'clock my flight time will be i see you at 5:00 PM ...bye...

Priya :- I am waiting for you ... welcome ...

(After talking to him, Priya immediately calls up Sub - Inspector shinde)

Priya :- hello sir ! Adv Priya this side ...

Sub inspector :- Yes ma`am! .... Tell me what happened?

Priya :- Our police department has been trying to catch a gangster named Nirvaan khan for many years...Today I am giving you that opportunity to catch that gangster (Nirvaan khan).

Sub-inspector :- (Shocked and curious) what...the Nirvaan Khan ...the gangster .. you are talking about ...

Priya :- Yes!... I am talking about that gangster, the Nirvaan khan, who was mastermind behind the plan bomb at Blue reddison Hotel ....He is coming to India from Dubai tomorrow, I will message you the place, where he going to meet me ...

Sub-inspector :- (excited and curious) ...Don't you worry ma'am, you just tell the name of the place, where he is going to be meet, I will reach with my police officer over there on time ....

Priya :- ok sir ... be ready to catch your prey(hunt)...

Sub – Inspector :- ok ma`am ,,, tommarrow we will reach there on time ...bye ....

CONCLUSION

The next day Nirvaan khan landed at airport in India around 4:00 PM and he called Priya and told that I have messaged the place name and address where we going to meet, I will be there in 30 minutes you too there soon, I am waiting for you

After that same address and place name Priya forward message to Sub - inspector shinde.

When Priya reached at decided place , she saw this is a big park. He (Nirvaan khan) was already sitting there...

Priya :- (totally blank) you reached before me, how long have you been waiting for me here...

Nirvaan :- (turn looking at Priya and smile) just reached 10 minutes before you ...

(Nirvaan Moves towards Priya and shakes hands with Priya)

Nirvaan :- (with hand shake) Hey

! its me Nirvaan Khan ...

Priya :- (smile) I know that ...hello

Nirvaan :- (continued)...I have to believe, it can be found only in India...

Priya :- (curious and smile) like what ...

Nirvaan :- (with smile) two lovers meeting in the park...(laugh) and the king lovingly called the queen and the queen, madly in love, ran to meet her king, without knowing the virtual intention of the king ...

Priya :- (shocked and looking at him)..what I didn't understand what you want to say..?

Nirvaan :- (he took out his gun and put it on Priya's head) I wish the queen will knew nature of king, before she fell in love with the king. But it's too late now .

Priya :- (panic and Cries) ..Please don't shoot, why do you want to kill me ?

Nirvaan :- (with smile and hold gun on her head) I have to kill you because it's part of my Nature, before any weakness overtakes me, before that I overtake the weakness...

(When police reach there, and police see Nirvaan has gun put on her head to shoot her, Seeing this, the police also surrounds Nirvaan from all sides and puts Gun on his head to kill him...and warns him that if he shoots Priya then the police will shoot him)

Policeman :- (warned)...don't shoot Mr Nirvaan...

(Nirvaana does not listen to the cops and shoots Priya on her head , and Priya falls to the ground and she is shot and dies there.)

As Nirvaan shoots Priya, in a hurry, the police also shoots at him, shoot a lot of bullets and he falls to the ground right there and and he die...

Both Priya and Nirvaan were lying dead on the ground.... The policemen picked up the dead bodies of both and took them to the grave for burial.

And the story ends by coming here that "Once there was the king, and the queen, both died the end of story"....

Contents

www.ingramcontent.com/pod-product-compliance
Lightning Source LLC
Chambersburg PA
CBHW021159130726
47988CB00004B/1688